To Papa

THE DRAGON FESTIVAL
by An Vrombaut
www.vrombaut.co.uk

First published in 2008 by Hodder Children's Books
First published in paperback in 2009

Text and illustrations copyright © An Vrombaut 2008

Hodder Children's Books
338 Euston Road, London NW1 3BH

Hodder Children's Books Australia
Level 17/207 Kent Street, Sydney, NSW 2000

ISBN: 978 0 340 93238 4
10 9 8 7 6 5 4 3 2 1

Printed in China

Hodder Children's Books is a division
of Hachette Children's Books
An Hachette Livre UK Company
www.hachettelivre.co.uk

The Dragon Festival

AN VROMBAUT

Hodder
Children's
Books

A division of Hachette Children's Books

Once upon a time there was a Princess ...

and her best friend was a dragon. But not just ANY dragon! Dear Dragon was a

bubble-blowing dragon,

which - according to Florrie - is the BEST kind of dragon of all.

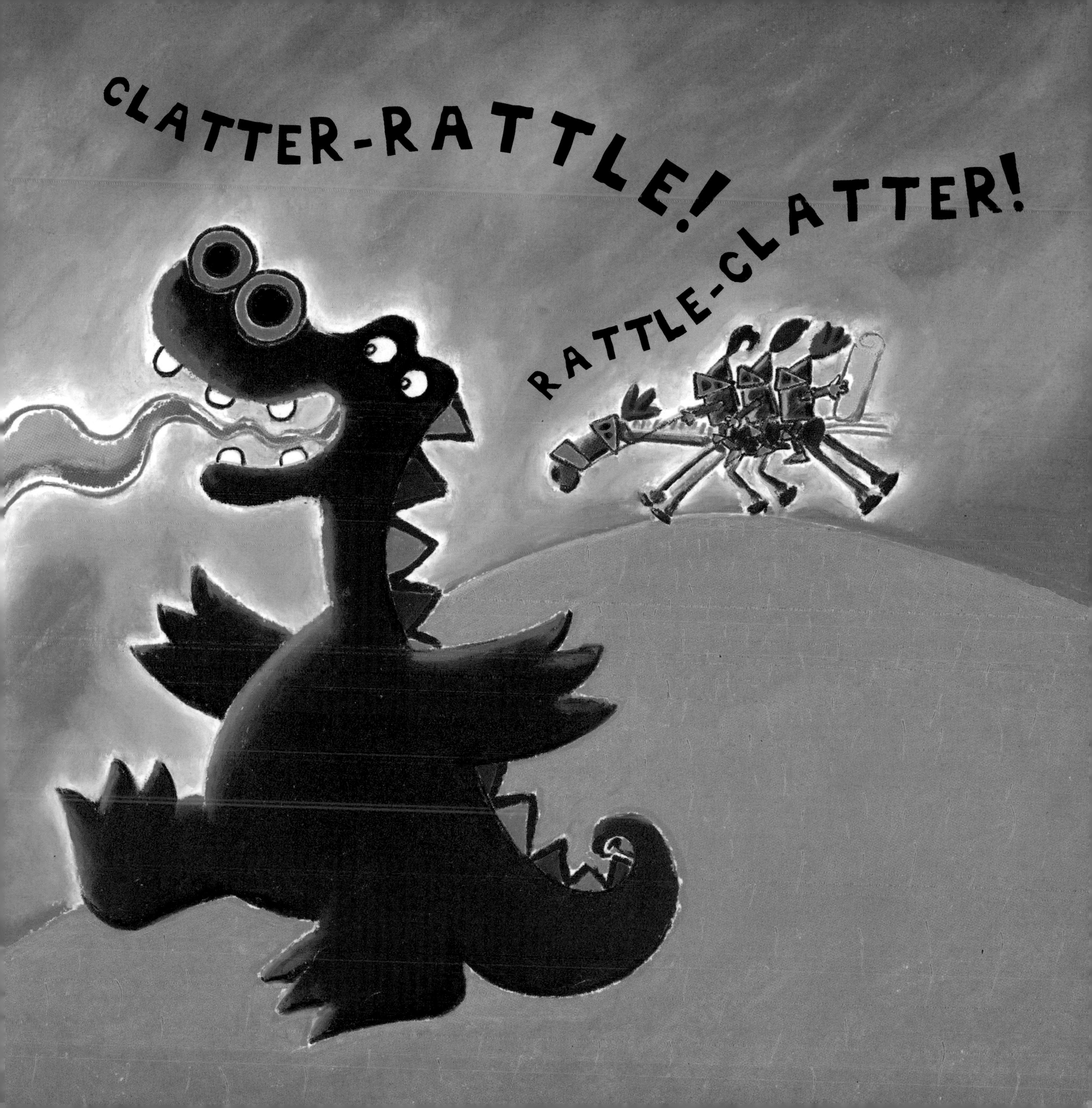
CLATTER-RATTLE!
RATTLE-CLATTER!

'HAVE YOU HEARD?'
shouted the knights.

'Heard what?' asked Florrie.

'About the
DRAGON
FESTIVAL!'

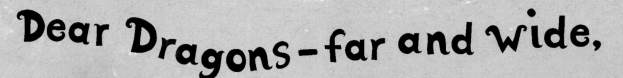

Dear Dragons – far and wide,

Come tomorrow to the Dragon Festival and join us in a dramatic display of Dragoneering.

May the best dragon win!

Thunderfangs – *the old and wise*

'How exciting,' said Florrie,
'Dear Dragon, you MUST take part!'

'But dragoneering means blowing fire,' sighed Dear Dragon. 'And you know I only blow bubbles. The other dragons will laugh!'

'Nonsense,' said Florrie.

But Dear Dragon was still worried...

The next morning dragons arrived from all over the land, flying and jogging and rollerblading. Florrie couldn't wait for the Dragon Festival to start.

Then **Thunderfangs** the old and wise stepped forward.

'Let the Dragoneering begin,' he said.
'Six cheers for the

Hexa-Dragon.'

'Let's hear it for the

Whirling

Twirling

Dragonettes.'

Get ready for **firework fun** with the

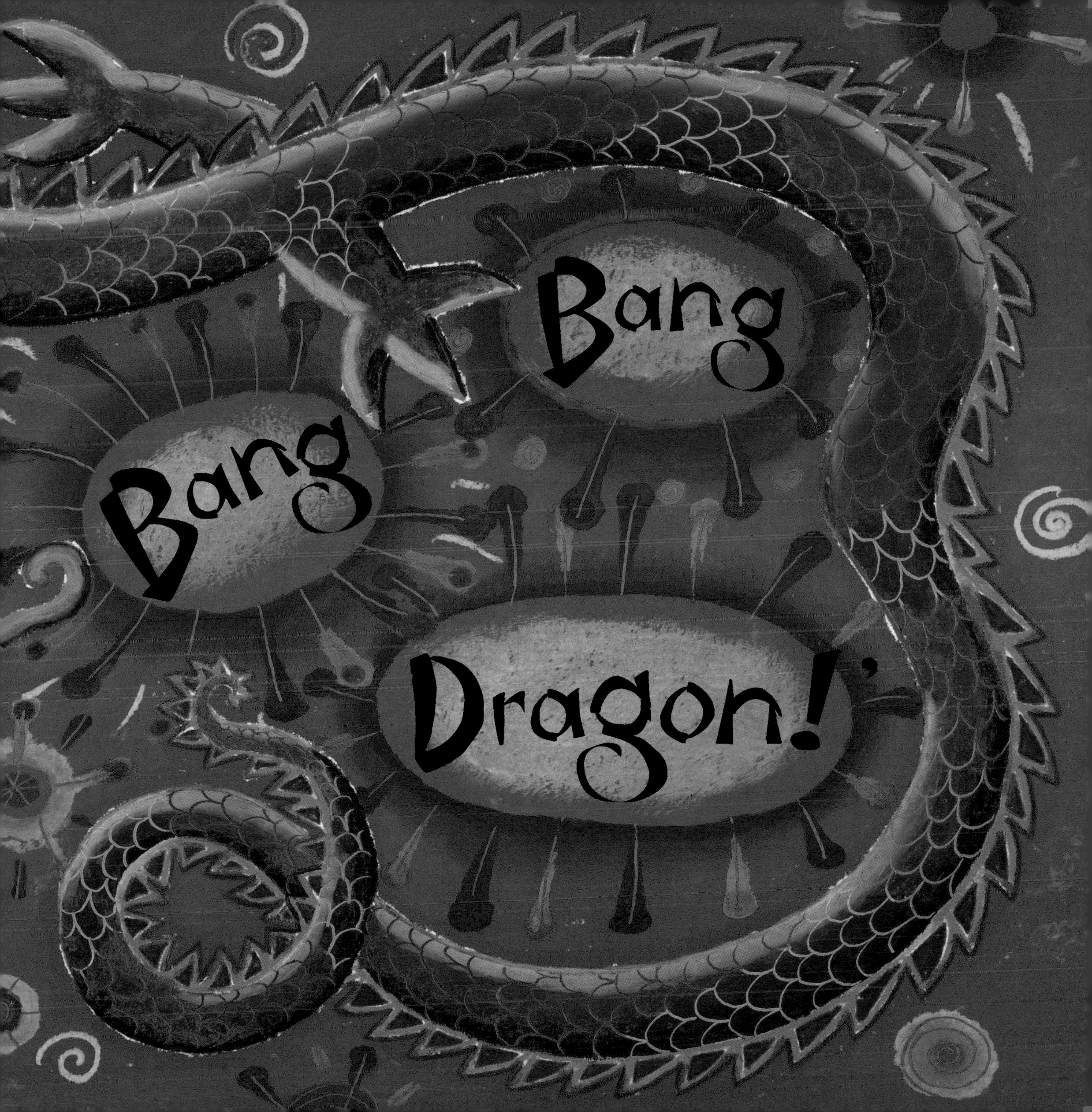

Bang

Bang

Dragon!'

'And finally,
introducing

Dear Dragon!'

But Dear Dragon was nowhere to be seen.
'Maybe he's run out of fire,' sniggered
the Bang-Bang Dragon.

'I'll find him,' said Florrie.

'PLEASE WAIT.'

Princess Florrie looked everywhere.

Dear Dragon wasn't under the rug.

Or in the kitchen.

Or up the cherry tree.

Finally she found him hiding in the maze.

'What's the matter?' asked Florrie. Dear Dragon sighed.
'I'm not really a dragoneering sort of dragon.'

'But you're Dear Dragon,' said Florrie,
'the best kind of dragon of all!'

Meanwhile, the dragons were getting grumbly. They wanted to know who had won the Dragon Cup.

'I bet it's me,' boasted the Hexa-Dragon.

'No, us!' the Dragonettes shouted.

He just took a **DEEP** breath and blew a
mountain of bubbles. Soon **ALL** the flames were gone.

'**Amazing,**'
shouted the
dragons.
'**HOW** did you
do that?'

'**IT'S DEAR DRAGON'S SECRET,**' said Florrie.

Thunderfangs nodded. 'Princess Florrie,' he said,
'why don't you present the Dragon Cup to the winner?'

Florrie smiled because
she knew exactly what to say.

'To Dear Dragon, the best kind of dragon of all!'

Other great Hodder picture books perfect to share with children:

978 0 340 88150 7

978 0 340 78859 2

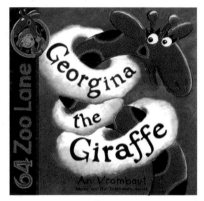

978 0 340 78861 5

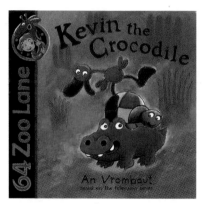

978 0 340 79562 0

978 0 340 85562 1

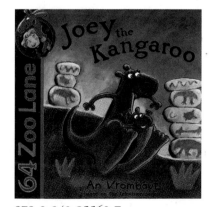

978 0 340 85560 7

978 0 340 79560 6

Hodder Children's Books

A division of Hachette Children's Books